PINKY CRASHES the PARTY!

Pinky CRASHES the PARTY!

By Michael Portis

Illustrated by Lori Richmond

Crown Books for Young Readers

New York

"What theme do you want for your birthday this year?" asked Penny's mom.

"A flamingo party!" said Penny.

"Who do you want to invite?" asked her mom.

"Pinky."

"We can invite your friends," said Mom.

"But not Pinky—he lives at the zoo."

"Pinky!" whispered Penny.
"You came for my birthday!"

"I'm going to the backyard," said Penny.

"You can stay for my party," said Penny, "as long as nobody sees you."

Penny went with her dad to buy supplies.

At the party store, she looked at balloons . . .

and piñatas.

At the bakery, Dad liked the simple cake.

Penny had other ideas.

"Do you like this one, Pinky?"

Dad's van was big enough to pick up all of Penny's friends.

At miniature golf,

the kids played every hole.

Dad played, too.

After golf, they headed to Penny's house for games and cake.

Mom put six candles on the cake. Dad added one for good luck.

They all sang, "Happy birthday, dear Penny . . ."

Then Mom and Dad handed out the party favors.

"Who's this?" Mom asked.

PINKY!

"Uh, we found your flamingo."

"Time to go home, Pinky."

For D.W. —M.P.

For the Dees, makers of the most
scrumptious birthday bakes —L.R.

Jacket art and interior illustrations copyright © 2020 by Lori Richmond

All rights reserved. Published in the United States by Crown Books for Young Readers,

an imprint of Random House Children's Books, a division of Penguin Random House LLC, New York.

Crown and the colophon are registered trademarks of Penguin Random House LLC.

Visit us on the Web! rhcbooks.com

Educators and librarians, for a variety of teaching tools, visit us at RHTeachersLibrarians.com

Library of Congress Cataloging-in-Publication Data is available upon request.

ISBN 978-1-101-93302-2 (trade) — ISBN 978-1-101-93303-9 (lib. bdg.) — ISBN 978-1-101-93304-6 (ebook)

MANUFACTURED IN CHINA

10 9 8 7 6 5 4 3 2 1   First Edition